The Fantastic Journey of PIETER BRUEGEL

BY Anders C. Shafer

DUTTON CHILDREN'S BOOKS · NEW YORK

To my great teachers—
Bob and Marty, Lester and Tom S.,
Uri and Donna

THE PUBLISHER AND AUTHOR WISH TO THANK THE FOLLOWING MUSEUMS, LIBRARIES,
AND PHOTOGRAPHERS FOR GRANTING PERMISSION TO REPRODUCE THESE WORKS
AND FOR THEIR KIND COOPERATION IN THE REALIZATION OF THIS BOOK.

Southern Cloister in a Valley, The Alchemist, The Beekeepers: © Kupferstichkabinett, Staatliche Museen zu Berlin—
Preussischer Kulturbesitz / photograph by Jörg Anders; *Mountain Landscape with River and Travelers*: © The British Museum,
London; *Big Fish Eat Little Fish*: Graphische Sammlung Albertina, Vienna; *Landscape with the Fall of Icarus*,
Fall of the Rebel Angels: Musées Royaux des Beaux-Arts de Belgique—Koninklijke Musea voor Schone Kunsten van België,
Brussels. © Photo d'Art-Kunstfoto Speltdoorn / photographs by Speltdoorn; *Dulle Griet*: © Museum Mayer van den Bergh,
Antwerp; *Tower of Babel, The Hunters in the Snow, The Wedding Banquet*: Kunsthistorisches Museum, Vienna;
The Wedding Dance: © 1984, The Detroit Institute of Arts, Detroit; *Land of Cockaigne*: Alte Pinakothek,
Munich / Bayerische Staatsgemäldesammlungen, Munich; *The Parable of the Blind*: Hans Hinz—Artothek /
Museo Nazionale di Capodimonte, Naples; *Summer*: © Hamburger Kunsthalle / photograph by Elke Walford;
The Magpie on the Gallows: Hessisches Landesmuseum Darmstadt

The illustrations for this book were drawn in pencil
and washed with watercolor and acrylic.

CIP Data is available.

Published in the United States 2002 by Dutton Children's Books,
a division of Penguin Putnam Books for Young Readers
345 Hudson Street, New York, New York 10014
www.penguinputnam.com
Designed by Amy Berniker and Ellen M. Lucaire
Printed in China
First Edition
1 3 5 7 9 10 8 6 4 2
ISBN 0-525-46986-9

Bruegel's Journey

MID-SIXTEENTH-CENTURY EUROPE

········· Bruegel's journey south
– – – – – Bruegel's journey back north

In sixteenth-century Europe, it was not unusual for painters from the north to travel to Rome in order to study Italy's great art and ancient ruins. A young draftsman and painter in his early twenties, whom we now call Pieter Bruegel the Elder and consider to be one of the geniuses of the Renaissance, set out from Antwerp on just such a trip in the mid-1500s. Bruegel left no written records of his trip—or of his life, for that matter. Only his artwork has come down to us. From his journey, a few drawings and later engravings survive, along with letters of contemporaries, to suggest where he went and what he saw. Surely his roughly two-year sojourn into foreign lands and across the Alps, during a period of religious persecution and violence, made a profound impression on the young artist. With careful regard for what is known of his journey, and from a life of looking at the art he created afterward, I have tried to imagine his experiences. I offer them here as a series of diary entries, along with my paintings of the scenes that go with them.

ANDERS C. SHAFER

SEPTEMBER 10, 1551

Shop of the Four Winds, City of Antwerp.

"You must decide soon, while there is still some warmth left in the season."

Master Hieronymous Cock, of the Shop of the Four Winds, is pressing me to make a trip south to the great city of Rome. He intends that I shall draw as I go and then study the arts and ancient ruins there. "The prints we make from the drawings you bring back will travel to the four corners of the world," he says.

It is late afternoon. I am dirty and tired, having spent the day pushing a stubborn knife through copper, engraving a picture of a castle. Now the autumn light off the sea bathes Antwerp in gold. I love this city, even when the winter wind sweeps its streets with ice. To reach Rome would take many months, perhaps a year or more. There are people here whom I would miss.

"Is Rome really so important?" I ask.

"It is not just Rome. It is the mountains you will pass through," Hieronymous says. "You're a lowlander. To see them with your own eyes will change you, Pieter."

"I have no horse," I remind him.

"I will find you a horse. And I will lend you money, maps. Go. Draw. You will return improved. Who knows what you may become."

SEPTEMBER 11, 1551

Shop of the Four Winds, City of Antwerp.

Today my head has cleared. How can I refuse to see this world
in all its good and evil?

"Don't go," the ink grinder says. "You'll be sorry." He is spin-
ning his mortar, making a deep sound. "Your road will be filled
with monsters most foul, bottomless pits, thieves of all kinds.
You will vanish beyond the hands of God—what will your
pretty lady do then?"

I have heard this idle chatter before. I tell him, "You, old
friend, you have spent all your years behind the city gates." But
in truth I am uneasy. These are dangerous times.

I make ink for the trip. I slip some fish guts into the soot and
oil to make the ink reddish, the way I prefer it. I must take care
to pack it far away from my biscuits. The ink smells like the
devil.

SEPTEMBER 20, 1551

A Field Somewhere South of Antwerp.

On my strong brown horse, I have ridden down through fragrant fields at harvesttime. The past days have been warm and the traveling easy.

Under the trees, peasants enjoy gruel and fruit, joking among themselves. I show them my drawings and laugh with them. I tell them my mother's old story about the delicious Land of Cockaigne. To get there, you have to eat through a wall of porridge three miles wide. But it's worth it because in that land the fences are made of sausage, the houses of cake. I tell them, "You should move there. You wouldn't have to work, just lie about, and the roast pigs will walk up to you and say, 'Here, take a bite of me.'"

Sadly, because of my excellent clothes, these peasants believe me to be in earnest. I find them friendly, direct, and truthful. Their rough, sturdy shapes are pleasing to draw.

City of Lyon, Kingdom of France.

I am spitting mad. I have come through a forest where thieves waited behind every tree, so I am drained of sleep from keeping an eye open all night. Then the toothless woman who pilots the ferry between Dijon and Lyon threatened to hurl me into the river if I did not pay her an exorbitant sum. She cheated me out of so much of my purse that I shall have to sell my horse. I had better master the French coins, or I will soon have to sell my beautiful coat.

   I can see that Lyon is built like a beehive, with many spiraling staircases. I hope to enjoy a meal of eel and warm bread at a good inn. They say that you must seize an eel by its head or it will forever slip away—like good fortune or a good start on a drawing.

OCTOBER 17, 1551

City of Lyon, Kingdom of France.

I see a play meant to teach people to be good. Doctors, merchants, cooks—all are reminded of their follies. The crowd prefers the clown to the other characters. They clap as he struts about the stage. I will use his mischief in my drawings. "How good to hear laughter," I say to the man beside me. In the name of religion, this countryside has revealed dark lessons. Yesterday Catholic soldiers were shoving a man with a bundle of straw on his back—probably a Protestant bearing the fuel with which he would be burned. I ask the man if he knows of this. "The Protestant said his faith in God would get him into Heaven faster than any amount of money he could give the Church," he tells me. "But we must not speak of it, or we, too, could be burned."

NOVEMBER 10, 1551

The Alps Mountains.

On a barge coming up a winding river, I see what I think are clouds. But as I walk up and up the steep paths, I find that the clouds are really snow on mountaintops. These are the Alps — great, high masses of rock under rolling skies. I see no belching fire, no devils, as the ink grinder foretold. Very cold, I wrap myself in blankets and build shelters out of stone to stop the wind. I have fallen many times but am only bruised.

One morning a band of boys awakens me. The large one has a crossbow. I think they seek to rob me. I order them away, and the big boy yells at the smaller ones, telling them where to run. Is it always the big fish that chase the smaller fish?

I am getting more accomplished at drawing mountains. I measure spaces between them with a stick and draw quickly with dots and lines so they look real to me. Mountains by other artists look like pretty pillows.

NOVEMBER 15, 1551 *The Alps Mountains.*

No monsters here, but thieves indeed on many paths. For protection I have taken on a companion I met at a crumbly inn. He is a blustering man with a rusty sword and a shield full of holes. As Hieronymous likes to say of some people, "He could dance under the gallows." The man looks unruly enough to keep passersby from peering over my shoulder, making suggestions how I might better draw this or that. If the blind lead the blind, both shall fall into the ditch, says the Gospel.

I here record a strange event. A team of small packhorses, led by men talking busily among themselves, passed us on a high, narrow road. As the last horse came by, it began to fall, scattering rocks and dust. I managed to pull it back, though pottery dropped out of its pack and crashed far below. I yelled at the men, but they simply kept on.

I like this gentle horse. It follows me now. I find it calms my fears of what lurks in these high places. I have been warned of bears and drunken soldiers.

An Alchemist's Home, the Piedmont, Far North of Rome.

After weeks of mud and snow, I wheeze and cough like a pig. But it is warmer here in this ancient town built high up on rocks. I think it is called Rivoli.

I rent a bed from an alchemist. Lice seem to be everywhere in his house. I pick them from my skin and clothes and can hear them marching around in my straw bed. The people here bathe only when the rain has filled their wells. I wish the wells were full more often. Children laugh when they catch me washing myself in a chilly fountain early in the morning.

The alchemist is trying to make gold out of cheap metal by using many steaming devices. I would tell him, if I could get his attention, that back in Antwerp we know you can't make gold out of metal. We say to people who think so, "All you will make is a quick trip to the almshouse."

I find it hard to draw because of the crowd, the noise, and the smoke. I would be more comfortable stabled with my horse. Even my companion leaves after a few nights. I must travel to a quieter place where I can sort out my drawings and try to understand what I have seen. The dizzying abysses. Plunging streams. The alchemist's sputtering machines and thick spectacles.

How strange but beautiful this world seems.

JULY 20, 1552

Reggio in Calabria

I have seized a chance to sail farther down the coast first, before Rome. I shall see that city later. Now I am at Reggio, a small city far south. Here I come upon a dark scene, a naval battle.

An old woman tells me that Ottoman soldiers are attacking, seeking rich Calabrian land and gold. They set Reggio on fire. I run down the street and hire a man who pilots a spice boat to transport me out of here—to anywhere. He must be crazed, because he sails the boat right into the battle. Ships crash into one another, cannons explode, men cry out, drown. Blood stains the water. I shake and feel sick.

Finally, we pass through the battle into a quiet expanse of sea. I look out at the vast mountains and cliffs, which stand silently over Reggio as if the battle weren't raging. I unwrap my papers and discover saltwater has ruined several drawings. My annoyance at this shames me, considering men are dying. I draw the land-scape, the burning town, noting the battle only with small dots and outlines, not wishing to dwell upon it. Then we sail south.

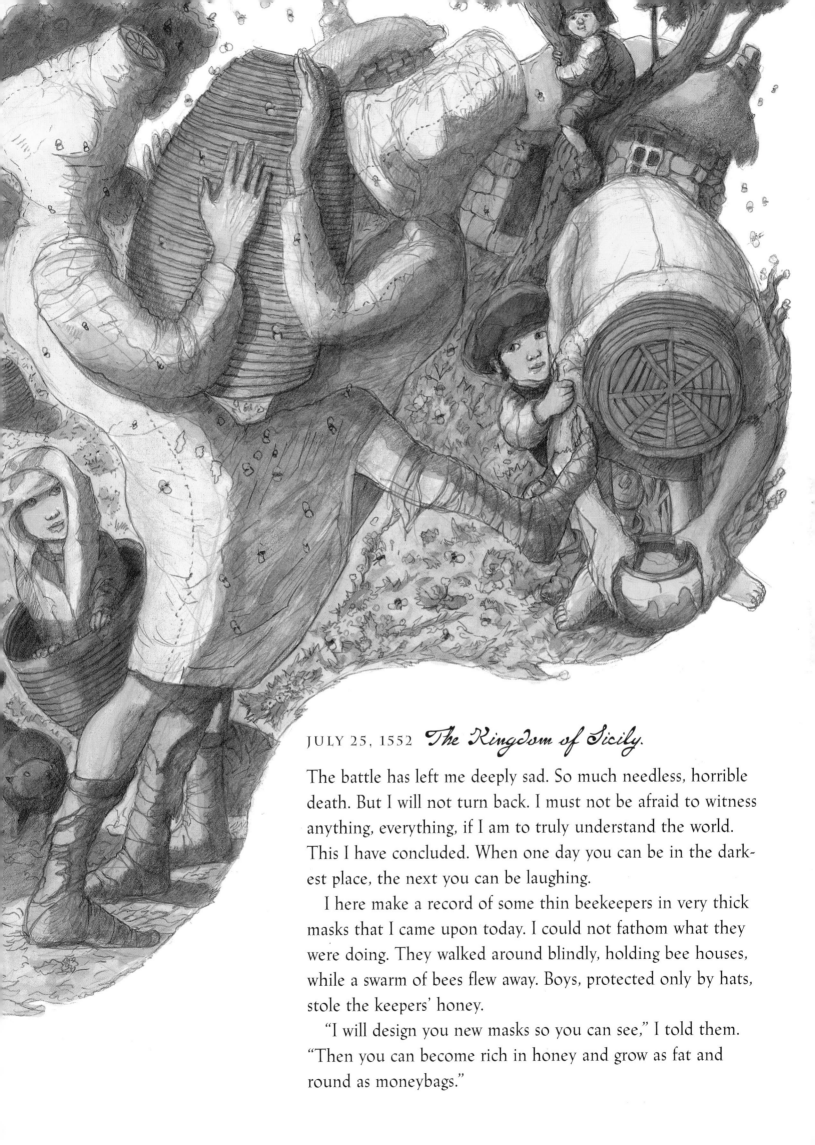

JULY 25, 1552 *The Kingdom of Sicily.*

The battle has left me deeply sad. So much needless, horrible death. But I will not turn back. I must not be afraid to witness anything, everything, if I am to truly understand the world. This I have concluded. When one day you can be in the darkest place, the next you can be laughing.

I here make a record of some thin beekeepers in very thick masks that I came upon today. I could not fathom what they were doing. They walked around blindly, holding bee houses, while a swarm of bees flew away. Boys, protected only by hats, stole the keepers' honey.

"I will design you new masks so you can see," I told them. "Then you can become rich in honey and grow as fat and round as moneybags."

SEPTEMBER 1, 1552 *Rome.*

At last, Rome. In this vast city, artists are at work everywhere.
I find a job in a church, high on a scaffold, painting trees into
the background of a work by an Italian master named Clovio.

The Romans are building many churches, filling them with
richly colored paintings that go all the way to the ceiling.
Antwerp has nothing like them. I think I can learn to draw like
the Italians, though they draw only figures, and I wish to draw
everything—trees, rocks, seas, and skies.

I am warmed by the voices in the streets, the laughter
of children, whose games are like those played in Antwerp.
Around each corner I find the smell of well-cooked food,
a small fountain in a square, a beautiful woman.

One day the great Michelangelo comes in to give us his
thoughts about our work. He draws and sculpts like an angel
but stinks like a monkey. His admirers follow him around,
some strutting like peacocks, but he pays no attention to them.
After seeing his work, I shall try to make my figures more solid
and rounded—more, as they say here, in the image of God.

SEPTEMBER 30, 1552 *Rome.*

Passing through a crowd of beggars, I hear angelic sounds and witness a great procession to celebrate a new saint. It is led by men carrying a stuffed white elephant adorned with golden flowers. Then come animals of all sorts, chained or in gilded cages. Big cats, monkeys, birds with giant beaks, even a stuffed rhinoceros. Soldiers in silver helmets follow on horseback, their bright orange banners snapping in the wind. Marching men beat on drums and blow horns. There are priests, cardinals with pointed hats, even the Pope. A traveler tells me the animals are the Pope's pets. Would that this might be the true and constant kingdom of heaven on earth, where soldiers march with shining horns, not swords.

I fill some days drawing ruins for the Shop of the Four Winds. I especially enjoy the remains of the old baths. Of their great arches, sufficient stone is left to produce an echo when I yell. The ancient stadium, covered with centuries of dust, is the largest I have seen. Here beggars dwell where once, I have heard, giant men fought lions to amuse the Romans.

A "rich kitchen" in a large home. Last night the owners asked Clovio and me to dine with other painters. We ate mountains of cheese and sat among meats dangling from the ceiling. All were invited to belch loudly, making a sound like thunder. How different from the poor kitchens where I ate on my trip here, where I searched and scratched in seashells for a little meat. I must admit the "rich kitchen" is the place for me, though the fat dogs howling at our feet reminded me of monsters.

OCTOBER 31, 1552

Just North of Rome. My Dream.

My dream. It must have been all the cheese. Monsters with familiar faces pursued me through a strange land. At the gates of hell, I came upon a woman called Mad Meg. She sat on a pile of treasures that she must have snatched from sinners on their way in.

"How do I get out of here?" I asked.

"Go see the king," she croaked.

With the monsters pulling on my clothes, I crawled over a hill and found a great tilting tower filled with workers chattering in different languages. A tall king stood giving orders, confusing his men, wrecking his cranes, causing his scaffolding to fall. To me, he said, "Go to the top of the tower, turn around twice, jump, and you're out."

I do not understand my dreams, but drawing them helps me. In a strange way, drawing what I cannot see shows me more truly what I do see.

JUNE 15, 1553
The Alps Mountains.

After nine months, I leave the hot crowds in Rome and go
north to cool, high places. I am at peace and love to draw in
the mountains, to describe with ink and chalk the endless
spaces, the tall magnificence, the curves that have rhythm like
a dance.

Here in a valley I find a camp with many sick people. A
beautiful woman and a man with long white hair walk among
them, providing food and water. Another man wears a mask
that looks like a wild boar. He believes it will frighten away the
demons that cause this plague.

As I pour water down a poor man's throat, the trees begin to
sway, then shake with sudden violence, spilling leaves and
twigs. The darkening sky hurls streaks of light and thunders
like cannon from a fleet of ships. Rivers appear from nowhere,
filling the paths. We rush to carry the sick to high ground and
cover them with leaves. Then the valleys become quiet, the
rocks dry. The trees stand still. Calm, I begin to draw. I thank
God that this plague has not invaded me.

After all this time in the mountains, I have begun to see
humankind as small and unimportant when compared with
such vast, stormy forces. Even our worries over heaven and hell
mean nothing in the face of this.

NOVEMBER 30, 1553

Breda. My Family Home. North of Antwerp, the Netherlands.

Throughout the two years of my journey, I have been yearning
to return to my boyhood home. I arrive on my little packhorse
from the Alps. Hunters come in with their dogs in the twilight.
Children play happily on the frozen lakes. I see warm fires in
the cottages, smell soup boiling, hear music. Dancing, singing,
great happiness.

My mother presents me with a new coat.

I will sleep for many days and nights, I am sure.

DECEMBER 23, 1553
Shop of the Four Winds, Antwerp.

I feel like skating down the frozen streams from Breda, so anxious am I to show Hieronymous my work. But I ride in on a wagon, then lay out my drawings. They cover the floor, and I must tack them all over the walls.

Hieronymous comes in and throws up his hands. I think for a minute he is disgusted, but he's not.

"These are worthy of a master. Worthy of a master," he repeats. "You have swallowed even the mountains and cliffs and spit them forth."

I blush deeply but am joyous.

1568 *Brussels.*

Many years have passed. I now prosper with a loving wife and two sons. I have a smooth stone house on High Street with five floors, many chairs, and a full cupboard. My firstborn likes to draw on everything, even the walls. Perhaps he will be an artist, too.

In each new work, I find the journey I took when I was younger. I saw then that people are given to much foolishness, cruelty, thievery, and greed, which we, as artists, must not turn away from. The madness is unceasing. Yet we must celebrate the glories, too. Not just the marble sculptures, paintings, and pageants of Rome, but the tall mountains, the wind that shakes the trees, our weddings and festivals, the rough peasant dances —and inside ourselves, what we dream, our laughter, our love for each other. All this we must now paint.

A Sampling of Pieter Bruegel's Art • The work of Pieter Bruegel that has come down to us consists of roughly sixty drawings and forty paintings, almost all of them done in the fifteen years after he returned from Italy. Much has been lost one way or another. Supposedly even Bruegel himself, on his deathbed, told his wife to burn some of his more satirical drawings, perhaps because he thought they would endanger her, given the climate of religious terror in which they lived. Bruegel died in 1569, in his very late thirties or early forties, "snatched away from us in the flower of his age," according to his friend the cartographer Abraham Ortelius.

Southern Cloister in a Valley, 1552.

Pen and brown ink with brown, pink, blue, and gray washes added by a later hand. 18.6 x 32.8 cm. Staatliche Museen zu Berlin, Kupferstichkabinett. KdZ 5537

Possibly only two drawings that Bruegel made from nature while on his trip survive. This is one of them, probably done in Italy. The quick dots and dashes he drew look as though they could have come from a modern artist. Bruegel signed it, suggesting he considered it a finished work, not just a sketch for reference.

Mountain Landscape with River and Travelers, 1553.

Pen and red-brown ink, with light wash. 22.8 x 33.8 cm. The British Museum, London

Probably thousands of sketches Bruegel made—on his trip and afterward, as studies for both prints and paintings—have been lost. This drawing was composed in a studio, from memory and perhaps from sketches. Scholars see in it techniques Bruegel absorbed from Italian artists such as Titian. The traveler on the left is pointing to a path that has been called the road of life.

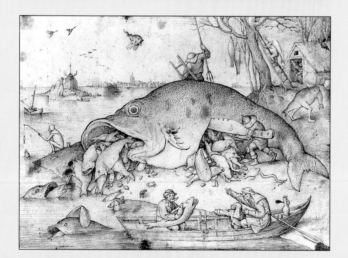

Big Fish Eat Little Fish, 1556.

Pen and brush and gray and black ink; 21.6 x 30.7 cm. Graphische Sammlung Albertina, Vienna 7875

This is one of the first of Bruegel's many drawings and paintings that illustrate proverbs and parables. People back then (as well as today) found in such pithy sayings a kind of ancient, thought-provoking wisdom. The huge fish seems to have died from eating too many little fish. Or is humankind also a big fish here?

The Alchemist, c. 1558.

Pen and brown ink. 30.8 x 45.3 cm. Staatliche Museen zu Berlin, Kupferstichkabinett KdZ 4399

Considered to be one of Bruegel's finest drawings, this, like many others, was intended to be the design for an engraving. In intricate detail, Bruegel shows the foolishness, disorder, and waste of the alchemist's attempt to turn cheap metals into gold. Beyond the window we see the final result of such behavior—a trip to the poorhouse.

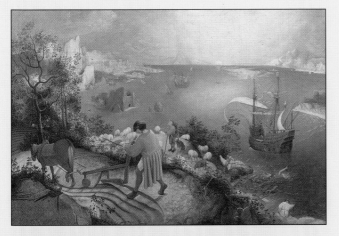

Landscape with the Fall of Icarus, c. 1558.

Oil on canvas. 73.5 x 112 cm. Musées Royaux des Beaux-Arts de Belgique, Brussels

The only painting of Bruegel's based on a Greek myth, this illustrates the story of a young man who flew so close to the sun that it melted his wax-and-feather wings. The landscape suggests Lake Geneva in the Swiss Alps. Here, when Icarus falls into the sea, only his splashing legs show. Nobody notices. A ship sails by without stopping. The farmer continues plowing. Icarus is just a ripple in the great world. W. H. Auden wrote about this painting in his poem "Musée des Beaux Arts."

Dulle Griet, 1562.

Oil on panel. 117.4 x 162 cm. Museum Mayer van den Bergh, Antwerp

This beautiful, scary, mysterious painting depicts the woman Dulle Griet, or Mad Meg, who, according to a Flemish proverb, "could plunder in front of hell and return unscathed." She profits from the sufferings of others, yet she appears to have a fierce, driving energy in the painting. The mouth of hell is part of a fantastical creature at the left.

Fall of the Rebel Angels, 1562.

Oil on panel. 117 x 162 cm. Musées Royaux des Beaux-Arts de Belgique, Brussels

Here, as in Christian legend, the good angels, led by the archangel Michael in armor, are casting out rebellious angels, like Lucifer, from heaven. As the angels fall, they become bizarre versions of the lower-order animals—strange reptiles, amphibians, insects, fishes—soulless, demonic creatures from hell.

Tower of Babel, 1563.

Oil on panel. 114 x 155 cm. Kunsthistorisches Museum, Vienna

This painting portrays the story in Genesis in which God punishes those who presume to build a tower to heaven by making them speak in different languages, sowing confusion and discord. Scholars believe Bruegel probably sketched the Colosseum when he was in Rome and referred to his sketches for this. Bruegel painted ruins into the tower so that it appears to have been built over centuries. He also shows the building techniques of his day in great detail.

Hunters in the Snow, 1565.

Oil on panel. 117 x 162 cm. Kunsthistorisches, Vienna

The colors in this painting from a series about seasons capture the way we feel and perceive on a cold winter day. Somehow Bruegel conveys even the feeling of biting, icy air. Perhaps for achievements like this, the mapmaker Abraham Ortelius said that Bruegel "painted many things that could not be painted."

The Wedding Dance, c. 1566.

Oil on panel. 119 x 157 cm. City of Detroit Purchase

Bruegel's first painting on the theme of peasants has a marvelous visual rhythm to it. Everyone seems to be hopping, bending, skipping, pushing, pulling in some fashion. The rich reds and whites bounce and weave. Bruegel tackled the problem of picturing movement in many of his paintings. He himself was most likely educated, but his paintings of peasants were so engaging that people called him "Peasant Bruegel."

Land of Cockaigne, 1567.

Oil on panel. 52 x 78 cm. Alte Pinakothek, Munich.
Bayerische Staatsgemäldesammlungen, Munich

The story of a wish-fulfilling land of plenty has been around in some form for a long time. Here a soldier, a peasant, and a clerk have eaten themselves into a stupor. A tree trunk supports a tabletop strewn with the remains of the meal. A pig conveniently has a knife stuck in its side as though ready for carving. But all this richness looks disturbing, too. Despite their fill, the people seem dull and empty.

The Wedding Banquet, c. 1567.

Oil on panel. 114 x 163 cm. Kunsthistorisches Museum, Vienna

Pudding is being served at this wedding feast. No matter where you look, each character is vividly depicted—the hungry bagpiper, the children licking their fingers, the men drinking or sipping. Everyone except the bride (in front of the green hanging) is intent on eating or drinking or conversation. Some scholars believe that Bruegel put himself in the picture—the bearded man at the far right, listening to the monk.

The Beekeepers, c. 1567–68.
Pen and brown ink. 20.3 x 30.9 cm. Staatliche Museen zu Berlin, Kupferstichkabinett KdZ 713

This enigmatic, arresting drawing has puzzled people for centuries. What is going on? Are those beekeepers or robbers? Has the boy in the tree found the honey first, or is he a lookout? Or is this an allusion to the Catholic Church, which in Bruegel's time was often compared to a beehive? The figure on the left bears a strong resemblance to one by Michelangelo in the Sistine Chapel, which Bruegel surely would have visited when he was in Rome.

The Parable of the Blind, 1568.
Tempera on canvas, 85 x 165 cm. Museo Nazionale di Capodimonte, Naples

Bruegel is illustrating verses from Matthew: "If the blind lead the blind, both shall fall into the ditch." Are the blind here nonbelievers, or are they Catholics and Protestants blindly leading each other to ruin in their religious wars? Bruegel observed so closely and painted with such vividness that modern doctors have been able to diagnose the different visual impairments of each man here.

Summer, 1568.
Pen and brown ink. 22 x 28.6 cm. Hamburger Kunsthalle, Kupferstichkabinett 21758

"Der Sommer" was in my parents' folio of prints that I saw when I was a child. The large, round figures show the influence of Michelangelo and suggest the plenty of summer, the feeling of working under a hot sun, the pleasure of quenching one's thirst. Some of the visual jokes create puns in the language Bruegel spoke.

The Magpie on the Gallows, 1568.
Oil on panel. 45.9 x 50.8 cm. Hessisches Landesmuseum Darmstadt

Flemish people thought a magpie resembled a "gossip" because of its chatter. And gossip was dangerous in Bruegel's time; religious persecution was swift and cruel. Are the dancing peasants oblivious to death and danger? The beauty of the landscape, of nature, dominates everything in the foreground. Do the magpie and the people represent but a brief moment, compared to the eternity stretching away behind them?

Author's Note
Author's Note

Bruegel left us only his art. What little we know of his life comes from accounts of his contemporaries or from those who gathered information about him in the decades following his death. We can more reliably trace the passage of his paintings from one collector to the next than we can construct a portrait of the man himself. Art historians have studied and restudied Bruegel's paintings and drawings to find clues to his originality, ideas, and genius.

Bruegel's birth is usually given as about 1525–1530, somewhere in the county of Brabant in the Netherlands. He lived most of his life around the cities of Antwerp and Brussels. According to a short biographical sketch by Karl van Mander, which appeared in 1604 and was probably embellished by hearsay, Bruegel studied painting in Antwerp with Pieter Coecke van Aelst, the court painter to Emperor Charles V. He is known to have painted the wings on an altar (now lost) for the glovemakers' guild in Mechelen. Sometime in 1550–1551, he was made a master in the Guild of St. Luke. Bruegel had a long connection with the engraver Hieronymous Cock, who ran the Shop of the Four Winds (*Aux Quatre Vents*) in Antwerp. Some art historians believe that Cock, who had himself recently visited Italy, supported Bruegel's trip to Rome so that he might return and make landscape drawings that could be engraved as popular prints. For about six years after his journey, Bruegel seems to have earned his living primarily from drawing landscapes, parables, and proverbs that other craftsmen could turn into engravings, etchings, and woodcuts. He worked closely with his engravers and may himself have learned that skill from Cock. In 1563, as he was painting more and more, he married Coecke's daughter, Maria Coecke van Aelst, and moved to Brussels. Most of his paintings that survive were accomplished in the last seven years of his life. Bruegel was friends with an urbane, literary class, and his commissions came from powerful merchants and officials. He died in 1569. His two sons, Pieter and Jan, also became painters.

Bruegel's century was a time of both abundance and upheaval in Europe. Antwerp, favorably situated for the new sea routes to Asia and America and north-south trade routes, grew and prospered. The wealth of its merchant community supported the thinkers and artists of the day. (In 1569, Antwerp had about one painter per 250 citizens.) Businessmen helped to finance the atlas of Bruegel's friend Ortelius, geographer to Philip II, the Spanish ruler of the Netherlands. But there was also a dark side: wars over territory and religion; hunger; poverty; plagues. The Catholic Inquisition was under way, attempting to halt the spread of Protestant reform by torture and death. Ortelius called it "a very disordered time." You can see the madness and stress in Bruegel's work. Yet he thrived. When Bruegel died, too young, Ortelius lamented that his death came because of "nature, who feared that his genius for dexterous imitations would bring her into contempt."

To create this book, I took a trip similar to Bruegel's, though by train, not by horse, boat, or on foot. Based on my reading and my own travels, I guessed that Bruegel left Antwerp in September 1551, to beat the winter; followed river routes on horseback and boat through Lyon, France, up to Geneva, Switzerland; and settled down for the winter in the Piedmont section of the Alps. Much speculation about his trip centers around a drawing he is thought to have done of the town of Reggio in flames, where a famous naval battle occurred in July 1552. I have him take a boat past Rome, leaving from Genoa and landing in Naples. Other authors suggest he left for Italy in 1552, took the Rhone River to Marseilles, then sailed to Naples and on to Reggio. I was surprised by the amount of contradictory information in my sources.

Until about one hundred years ago, Bruegel was thought of chiefly as a painter of peasants. We now know that his work covers hundreds of subjects, almost like an encyclopedia of human understanding for his time. He did not portray an idealized, mythic, or aristocratic world, but turned to everyday people and things. He used old parables, Bible stories, proverbs, landscapes, seasonal activities to reflect on human nature, but his art went way beyond simple moralities. His renderings of people allow us to feel an individual's intention and energy, to see through to a soul's happiness or confusion, fear or disappointment, greed or meanness, isolation or joy. I believe Bruegel's trip deeply influenced him—not just the art, ruins, and mountains, but the opportunity to experience the wide world and reflect profoundly on its vastness and variety, and also on its universal aspects. In his work you find insights into human needs, failures, triumphs, love; into people's fascination with their bodies and imaginations; into illnesses, crimes, justice. And you see a powerful comprehension, new for his time, of our great natural surroundings and how we fit in them. Some of it is indeed funny, grotesque, wild. All of it contains many levels of significance, arranged in brilliantly organized, richly detailed compositions.

I first saw his work in an old cardboard folio of prints in my parents' library when I was very small. His imagination gave impetus to my own. I have never stopped looking. His trenchant, intuitive grasp of human life speaks to us still. His narratives can be witnessed every day. Beauty never dies.